W9-DEE-303

FV.

WITHDRAWN

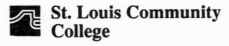

COWBOY NIGHT
BEFORE CHRISTMAS

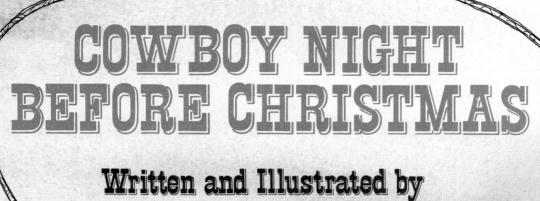

COWBOY NIGHT BEFORE CHRISTMAS

Written and Illustrated by
JAMES RICE

Formerly Titled
Prairie Night Before Christmas

PELICAN PUBLISHING COMPANY
GRETNA 1993

First printing, 1986
Second printing, 1990
Third printing, 1993

This book is a reprint of *Prairie Night Before Christmas* © 1986.

Library of Congress Cataloging-in-Publication Data

Rice, James, 1934-
   [Prairie night before Christmas]
   Cowboy night before Christmas / written and illustrated by James
Rice.
    p. cm.
   Originally published: Prairie night before Christmas. 1986.
   Summary: When Santa's reindeer abandon their job in the midst of a
Texas storm, he enlists the help of two lonely cowpokes so that he
can finish his Christmas Eve rounds.
   ISBN 0-88289-811-6
   1. Santa Claus--Fiction. 2. Cowboys--Fiction. 3. Christmas-
-Fiction. 4. Texas--Fiction. 5. Stories in rhyme. I. Title.
PZ8.3.R36Co   1990
[E]--dc20
                                90-7280
                                 CIP
                                 AC

Printed in Singapore

Published by Pelican Publishing Company, Inc.
1101 Monroe Street, Gretna, Louisiana 70053

'Twas a cold Christmas eve
  on the Southwestern plain
And the North wind was blowin'
  through a broke winderpane.

In that sod shanty shack
  far from home, warmth and care
Shivered two lonely cowboys,
  such a scraggly pair.

They crowded the farplace
    where the flames flickered low
From smoldering embers
    that heated too slow.

Then a knock at the door
    and a bang on the wall—
Over the sound of the storm
    they heard a voice call,

"Please open the door
    and let me come in;
I'm near froze to death
    and chilled to the skin."

The door was unbolted
    and then opened wide
And a fat li'l ole man
    jumped quickly inside.

There was frost on his whiskers
    and ice hung from his nose;
He shivered and shook
    from his head to his toes.

In spite of discomfort
    he didn't complain.
His expression was jolly
    as he paused to explain,

"I was movin' this cargo
    and making good time;
I'd covered the country
    from desert to pine,

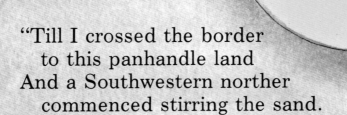

"Till I crossed the border
     to this panhandle land
And a Southwestern norther
     commenced stirring the sand.

"The temperature dropped
     more'n a hunnert degrees;
My team soon fled North
     where they'd less likely freeze."

The old cowman had doubts
    'bout the strange little man
But in Southwest tradition
    he put out his hand.

"You can shake off your boots;
    you're welcome to stay
Or we can help ya
    to be on your way."

The answer came quickly
    with a twinkle of eye,
"I got many a mile yet
    'fore the sun hits the sky.

"Could you find me a team
    (I gladly will pay)
Then point my nose South
    and I'll be on my way."

"The only critters we have
    that could pull a full load
Are the ornery longhorns
    and they'd have to be showed.

"They ain't ever been hitched
    to a wagon with reins;
They'd be too much trouble—
    they're a mite short on brains."

They made an odd threesome
as they went out on the range—
The old cowhand and the youngster
and the old man so strange.

They saddled three broncs
    in the dark freezing night;
With cold-stiffened fingers
    they made the cinch tight.

While roping the longhorns
    they bumped and they stumbled
And numerous times
    from their hosses they tumbled.

It took all three working
an hour or more
To hitch up the wagon
in two rows of four.

The longhorns at first
refused to obey,
When the strange little man
tried to get under way.

Then one lifted his head
and gave out a bellow
And the rest one by one
they started to follow.

The longhorns were straining
and pulling together;
they built up their speed
then just like a feather—

On a strong gust of wind
  their feet gave a bound
Then man, wagon and longhorns
  all at once left the ground!

The old cowboy and youngster
  stared up in surprise,
A trick of the storm,
  too much wind in the eyes—

Those were their thoughts
as they looked at the sky;
Any fool knew darn well
that such things cannot fly.

The young cowboy grumbled
   as they moved toward the shack,
But the old one stayed quiet
   pert' near all the way back.

They reached the sod shanty
and opened the door
And they couldn't believe
what they saw on the floor.

Two pairs of new boots
   with spurs made of silver,
With a note but no clue
   as to who was the giver.

They made out the words
   in the dim farplace light:
"MERRY CHRISTMAS TO ALL
   AND TO ALL A GOOD NIGHT!"